SIBERIAN STOWAWAY

SIBERIAN STOWAWAY

By

Constance W. Langtry

ISBN: 0-75960-071-6

1stBooks - rev. 11/2/00

FOREWORD

This story was first conceived in a file folder labeled, "The Book," in 1970. It later became a copyrighted autobiography, *A Russian Mascot in the U.S. Army,* in which my husband, Alec Langtry, covered the years 1918-1922. In 1976, after he had been to Russia with our daughter, Sondra, he taped orally those experiences and former ones.

Meanwhile, Sondra wrote a journal, *Back to the U.S.S.R.,* covering her trip in 1976 from Egypt, through Russia, to Japan. Parts of her work are incorporated in *Siberian Stowaway.* Furthermore, many letters from the 1920s were a source of my information for the copyrighted manuscript.

Neither my husband, nor my daughter, is alive to receive my profound gratitude for their contributions to this book. Without them, this fascinating story could not have been written.

PART I

THE BRIDGE IS BROKEN

CHAPTER 1

The Russian captain and I are on the bridge of his Soviet ship as it moves slowly toward the Eisenhower Locks at Massena, New York. I am piloting the ship from Cape Vincent through the Thousand Islands in the sparkling St. Lawrence River. To pass the time, I open the conversation.

"I was born in Russia - Khabarovsk in the Russian Far East. I left there in 1919 and lost touch with all members of my family after 1922. Unfortunately, I can remember very few Russian words and can't speak or write sentences."

"I can give you an address for an office in Moscow," responds the helpful captain, "that has located the families of some foreigners." He writes the address in English.

"You are the only Russian who has given me a real lead in this regard," I continue. "I knew several Russian pilots on the Suez Canal when I was there from 1956 to 1964, but we talked more about money and general conditions than about my lost relatives."

"How did you like it?"

"It was the most interesting and challenging experience of my life. I worked in the harbor where I handled over 5000 ships from all nations entering from the Mediterranean. The international group that answered the need for pilots when President {Gamal Abdul} Nasser nationalized the canal in July 1956 was not concerned about Nasser's politics or that of other pilots – only money. But with the special training required and a canal blocked with damaged ships after the Seven-Day War, now almost forgotten, it took us licensed captains over a month to qualify. There were a lot of parties given by the councilor offices of different countries in Port Said, – I remember especially those of yours and mine. I think you would have liked it." (He was about twenty years younger than I.) We laugh together as I climb down the ship's ladder with the words, "See you in the USSR." And I could at least say *spasee ba* (thank you) with confidence and sincerity.

As soon as I arrive home after this assignment, I excitedly show the address to my wife, Con, and daughter, Sondra. Then I rummage through a drawer of old letters from the early 1920s that give the names of my parents, three brothers and four sisters. After reading these letters, several translated from the Russian and others explaining my early life, Sondra, who was continuing to study the Russian language and had spent a summer at the University of Leningrad, composed a letter for my signature. She had been urging me to continue my search "before you are older and grayer."

The letter, dated October 13, 1973, began, "I have been told that you may be able to help me in a matter very dear to my heart," a not-so-subtle sentimental appeal to the unknown Russian reader. Facts regarding my family gleaned from the letters were given for identification.

Two months later, I hurry home after taking an envelope from my post office box with an unfamiliar and beautiful Russian stamp. The note card picturing snow-covered evergreen trees has the message typed in Russian. For translation, it goes to Sondra who is living in Washington. When she returns it, I read:

Head of the Search Department of the Executive Committee of SOKK
(SOKK may be short for Soviet Control Committee)

Dear Aleksandr Andreivich:

We received your letter but unfortunately we are unable to grant your request for our committee is not involved in searching for people.

We recommend that you once again turn to the Red Cross {I had tried the American Red Cross in 1939} with this request. In your letter by all means, give all the facts. We give you the address of the Red Cross (in Cyrillic).

We wish you success. May I take this opportunity to wish you all the best in the New Year, 1974, Signed A. H. Konyaev
December 30, 1973 Moscow

In accordance with his suggestion, a duplicate letter is sent to the Red Cross in Moscow, Meanwhile, I retire from the St. Lawrence Seaway but continue to live in Cape Vincent.

Two years pass; August 1975 - a telephone call from the nearest city, Watertown: "Mr. Langtry, this is the American Red Cross I am forwarding a letter today from our Washington headquarters." It comes. Impatiently, I read:

Will you please advise Mr. Langtry of the following report: Antonina (Tonya) Andreyevna Struchkova (b.1907) lives at . . . Khabarovsk; Anastasiya (Asya) Andreyevna Struchkova (b. January 17, 1916) lives at . . . Kiev. Andrei Filippovich Struchkov (father) died in 1943; Pelagaya Ivanovna Struchkova (mother) died in 1953; Mikhail (Misha) Andreivich Struchkov died in 1938; and Valentina (Valya) Andreyevna Struchkova died in 1931.

The local Red Cross representative has added, "We hope this information will be helpful to you." What an understatement!

I write immediately to Tonya, hoping against hope that this will bridge a time-span of fifty-five years and confirm our identification.

The answer in a clear, bold hand, speaks for itself as dimming memories become fresh when translated from Russian:

My dear and own brother Shura:

You cannot imagine what happiness your letter brought me. I, not having opened it (having forgotten the heaviness of shoulders that 68 years can give) broke into a dance. I remember everything. . . .

Then I unsealed your letter and a wave of memories of childhood rushed out – everything. . . .Where, oh where is that dear childhood your letter brought back into my soul and memory . . .

All do visit and fish in the Amur. Visit! We will greet you with our nice Russian custom, bread and salt, and huge Russian hugs.

I will reread her letter often; there is much more to digest. One sad item was the death of my older brother, Ivan, in 1975, whom I missed contacting by a few months. My oldest sister, Motya, lives near Tonya. My youngest sister, Asya, writes with an invitation to visit; her recollections of me are based on those of older family members.

I am determined to visit my three sisters.

Spring 1976; Wilmington, North Carolina, my new address. At the desk of my travel agent, I say, "I want to go to Khabarovsk." When I mention the location of the city, new to him, he lifts a heavy book from a shelf, listing airline schedules, including that of Aeroflot, the Soviet airline. The tickets are for departure on the first day of September, the easiest part of the arrangements..

What red tape! First, the application for the Russian visa has to be requested from the Russian Embassy in D. C. if you are an American citizen, no matter where you live; it has to be completed in Russian and English. The most important question of many is, "Why did you leave Russia?" Without hesitation, I write the truth: "I left without parents' permission." It allows me to return with no hassle.

The family translator, Sondra, is living temporarily in Cairo, Egypt, and will also go to Russia, but Con, my wife, chooses to visit her only sister in Minnesota during my absence.

The paperwork, including special invitation forms from two sisters, seems overwhelmingly complicated. But finally I have all the documents required for the journey and so does Sondra in Cairo.

Because we know Russian living-space is limited, it is decided that Sondra, will visit first her aunt Asya in Kiev. She will leave by ship from Alexandria for Odessa; then fly to Kiev. We will eventually meet in Khabarovsk at Tonya's apartment.

CHAPTER 2

September 1, 1976. Up at 5:00 am in Cape Vincent. Con and I arrive at the Watertown airport for the seven o'clock Piedmont flight to Washington.

On arrival, I am off on my own as she goes her way for her Minnesota flight.

"Here are a pack of souvenir cards from Piedmont," says the pretty stewardess as we are off for JFK airport. She then confides, "I'm caught in a bind. Never a life of my own. I'm off as soon as I land. How can you make friends that way?" Her question goes unanswered as a buzzer sounds and she walks down the aisle to investigate.

At the Piedmont terminal, I must find my way to Pan Am. The airport with its circle of airline alphabets and maze of roads is mind-boggling. With hours before my overseas flight, I prefer to walk rather than wait for the shuttle-bus. Dragging my luggage carrier with its one suitcase, and with my waterproof LL Bean knapsack on my shoulder, I start. Coming toward me is a young man, trundling his bag.

"Which way is Pan Am?" I ask.

"You're going in the wrong direction. It's 'way over there." He points a half-mile away.

"That's quite a walk. I'm going to rest here on the curb."

"Good idea. Mind if I join you?"

As we sit by the road, I ask, "Where are you from?"

"Israel. I'm checking out a couple of universities here in the U.S. I was born in New York City."

"I've never been to Israel, but I can't help thinking how much has changed in the Middle East since I left Egypt in 1964. I know you're too young – or not even born – to remember the Seven-Day War in 1956. The way nations are lined up now, it was strange that the U.S. and the Soviet Union were opposing France and Britain."

"You're right about my lack of knowledge on that score."

"Last winter," I continue, "I returned to Egypt and met some former colleagues. That was fun. But when bombs fell in that war twenty years ago, a bomb destroyed my room in a well-built apartment on the Port Said waterfront. A narrow escape. But no place is safe in any kind of war."

"Wish I could hear more," says my new friend as he stands up, "but my plane might leave without me." .

With a handshake, we walk in opposite directions.

The ticketing girl stands alone at the Pan Am counter. “You have a four-hour wait for your 044 flight to Moscow, but I can take your bag off your hands and put it behind the counter. Don’t tell anyone because I’m not supposed to do this. Your flight won’t be called for three hours and a half; that’s a long time to drag a bag around.”

“Thanks a lot. I’m not one for sitting still long so you’re doing me a big favor.”

A cup of coffee at a snack-bar hits the spot.

In a secluded spot, I reread Tonya’s year-old letter giving her last memories of me:

“It was August 1919. A sunny day, early evening about four or five o’clock. I asked Mama permission for a glass of cherry syrup and I received her permission. I took it correctly, not wetting my fingers. (The syrup was in a large kettle.) You, looking at me, also asked permission for the syrup and Mama didn’t refuse you. But you didn’t hold the glass of syrup carefully and plunged your arm up to the elbow into the kettle and took out your arm from the kettle. But how? All red from the syrup. I started jumping for joy for what you were going to get from Mama. Mama scolded you a bit and then began to laugh. Your feelings were hurt and you said, ‘How come your Tonya can do everything and I can’t do anything?’ You went out. You didn’t come back for the whole evening. We all started to worry, particularly Mama. Then you came back. So that is the last event from your childhood and how many times there were."

"Flight 044 now boarding for Moscow via Copenhagen." Welcome words over the loudspeaker, It is 7:35 pm. I line up with others, including groups of grandmas – babushkas – returning to Moscow from where?

As I enter the Boeing 747 with no seats assigned, I survey this flying football field and take a seat on the aisle in order to stretch out for sleep on the inner ones. But, no luck. A whiskered young man chooses the window seat. He's headed for Hamburg, Germany, he tells me.

"I haven't been there for years. I was a young A.B. (Able Seaman) on one of those huge passenger ships, either the *America* or the *Leviathan."*

"I'm going as a deck-hand on a small, sailing vessel like those you see advertised as Windjammer cruises for parties in the Caribbean. I'm meeting the captain in Hamburg. He's only twenty-five. (My seat-mate was perhaps twenty.) But I really want to learn navigation."

"I can tell you one thing. If you have a sextant and keep your eye on the polar star, the angle above the horizon will give you the latitude. But that's only the beginning."

As we float through the dark, Walt and I touch many subjects in our conversation.

"At fifteen, I left my parents and junior high school – Joel Chandler Harris – in San Antonio. I still have my yearbook; listed in the class prophecy as editor-in-chief of the Salt Lake City *Desert News* (I probably talked with pride of my days delivering *The Deseret News*.). I have a laugh when the shipping agent in Vera Cruz for my first job, mess boy, asked my birthplace, spelled Utah, E-U-T-A-H.

"You're about the age I was when an older brother, answering a letter of mine, wrote from another country where he was studying, 'What do you mean by been to sea? Is it to study, to work or the trips to Germany?' Then he refers to an aerial school I had written him about.

"In Lincoln, Nebraska, at age twenty, I paid two hundred dollars for ten hours of flying instruction. One day the instructor had gone off, leaving the class of ten up to no good. Without permission after several lessons, I took a plane up alone. Somehow I escaped wires and railroad yards, and brought the plane safely to rest in a farmer's hayfield; no hidden rocks and no dips. The fascination with flying has never left me and I have a few more hours officially added to that first recorded solo.

"But my brother cannot understand why I jump from one thing to another. He foresaw realistically and correctly that without special education, my road would be 'very, very hard and slow.'"

Walt and I try to sleep in uncomfortable positions. Finally, the sun is flooding the small window. A wake-up towel is offered. "We are arriving at Copenhagen airport," come the words over the loudspeaker. "This is a one-hour stop while we change to a 707, a smaller plane. Copenhagen time is 7:30. You may take a little walk around the airport. Do not leave anything in the plane."

"Goodbye, Walt. Good luck on the cruise."

I leave for the tax-free shops with other passengers. I see the airport name is Kastrup Lufthaus. On the walking sidewalk, I move with other people for about fifteen minutes. In front and behind me are children, men and women, old and young, trundling bicycles. It's as if they were born with bicycles. This must be a short cut; certainly they are not all passengers.

After a quick look around, I return to the plane; an aisle seat again as we load for Moscow. A middle-age couple stash their coats and small parcels overhead. He sits next to me.

"How far are you going?" I ask.

"Mary and I are scheduled for a cruise on the Volga. I was born in Russia but this is her first visit. I met her in the Philippines when she was with the U.S. State Department and I was a mining engineer there. During World War II, I hid out from the Japanese in the Philippine mountains. What is your destination?"

"Khabarovsk, where I was born," I reply.

"I have been there many times and know it well."

Surprising! Never had I met anyone who knew my birthplace, not to mention having been there. Immediately I am on a first-name basis with Mike and Mary.

We share knowledge of two places in common: the Philippines and Russia.

"Manila," I begin, "was where I arrived on the troop ship, *Great Northern,* in 1920. I was eleven. It took seven days from Vladivostok. As soon as the ship docked, a Private, Clair Scott, buttonholed a reporter for the *Manila Tribune* who was wandering around the ship. He said, 'I've got a story for you if you walk off the ship wih a kid.'

"'Come on, kid. Where'dya come from?'

"'Vladivostok.' We walk down and off the gangway. Then he tells me, 'Manila's a fine place, but lotsa kids like you are put in a compound and sent back.' I am stunned! That fact has never occurred to me. Finally, he takes me to the central plaza where the troops are waiting for the next orders.

"After a few days with my army friends in their barracks, I'm written up in the *Tribune*: a mysterious Russian youngster in a little American army uniform, who speaks a few words of English.

"Next I'm in a mansion like nothing I had ever seen. A photo album has refreshed my few memories of a short stay. Inscribed 'To Alex, from Daddy and Mama Perkins, Manila, P.I., August 20, 1920,' its pictures are of a veranda around a large one-floor house with an overhanging tree, an airplane, a touring car, a swimming pool with adults lined up in what look like sleeping garments, and a handsome horse with a handsome woman rider. But the most intriguing picture is one of myself in a white suit, matching shoes and socks, standing beside a little girl in party dress. The idea of a brother for the little girl was short-lived. It is back to the barracks for me."

Over the loudspeaker, "We will be arriving in Moscow in five minutes. Moscow time is noon. The temperature is 60 degrees Fahrenheit."

Our reminiscences about the Philippines, even though about twenty years apart, make the two hours to Moscow pass like two minutes.

"Alec," says Mike, "we have so much more to talk about – our stories of Russia and the Philippines. Palm Beach where I live and your home in Wilmington are not far apart. We'll keep in touch and get together." And we do.

CHAPTER 3

Sheremetyevo! The largest of three airports in Moscow. It's like trying to navigate the Zambesi River without a compass.

First is Passport Control where I present my visa and passport. The young officer in his dark green uniform with red piping on cuffs, collar and cap glances at my face to see that it agrees with my self-conscious grinning likeness. Stamping only my visa for a four-month stay – I will stay one – he returns both documents with the flicker of a smile. As the visa mentions my birthplace as Khabarovsk – the passport, Russia – I can imagine he is wondering how an American citizen with the name, Alec Langtry, was born in that city in 1909,

My mind goes back to my first passport picture, safely at home. Four serious faces: Mae Langtry, "mother," with a simple, brimmed hat, Otto James Langtry, "father," with a smooth, thin face and two boys with proper neckties on their white shirts: a 14-year-old son, Cleon, and me, the 12-year-old new son. The faces in the photo are as clear as in 1921.

How come I am the fourth member of the Langtry family?

One February day I am standing in front of the garage of the Motor Transport Detachment, U.S. Army, in Manila. A tall, lanky officer comes up to me. I spy a gold leaf on his shoulder. Later, I learn that it signifies he is a major.

"I have seen you around here every day for some time. Where do you sleep?"

"Here in the barracks," I answer.

"I saw you get off the ship with the soldiers. Where is your home?"

:"Khabarovsk."

"Where is that?"

"On the Trans-Siberian Railroad," I reply.

"Does your family know where you are?"

"No. But Mama said I could go with the soldiers." Up to this time, I had told all inquirers that I was an orphan.

"What does your father do?" was the Major's next question.

"In the station of the railroad – baggage and other things."

Both the Major and I make inquiries separately. He knows I am called Alek and I know he is Otto James Langtry of the Quartermasters Corps.

Shortly after our conversation, he invites me to lunch and to meet his wife at his quarters. At once, Mrs.Langtry offers to help me with English lessons. Thereafter, I have lunch with them daily and word drills: "bohl," Alek, "not bawl." And so it went.

But the day comes when I do not show up for lunch. Where can he be? Maybe he has had an accident? No sight of him since nine o'clock the previous night.

Major Langtry rounds up a search party. Around midnight, "Here he is!" Happily and naturally, in the amusement park near the Ferris wheel. I explain that once the operator had given me a free ride and I was waiting for another one. It was an enchanting place with its bright, dazzling lights. To think that anyone would be concerned about my disappearance was something new. But after that episode, Major Langtry laid down the law. No more sudden disappearances; tell either me or Mrs. Langtry where you are going.

Now I am sleeping as well as eating at the Langtrys. Their household includes their son in the passport picture, and teenage Steban, a Filipino all-around servant. I get to know him well as my role overlapped his. Because army protocol demands much entertaining, which the Langtrys seem to enjoy, there are many dinner parties and formal teas. Table-setting and dish-washing without end! When Mrs. Langtry says, "I will wash the stem glasses with the gold bands," both Steban and I are relieved. (I still use that glassware and the beautiful blue and white china with its flowery tree design and the tiny Fuji on the bottom.) I had known informal hospitality only.

However, I dread the "teas." I try to be out of the house, if possible; otherwise Mrs. Langtry introduces "our little Russian boy." What am I supposed to do? At the time I do not realize that everything I am learning in this new culture will be invaluable as I live life.

At the end of the 1920 summer – August 17, to be exact – I am Alec Langtry. A legal document appoints "O. J. Langtry, by profession a Major, the guardian of Alexander Struchkoff." It is issued by "The Court of First Instance of Manila, United States of America, Philippine Islands."

"Have you adopted me?" I ask.

"A lawyer tells me I cannot adopt you because I do not have your parents' permission. You say they are living in Khabarovsk, but I cannot get in touch with them because of the revolution, and anyway I never heard of that city."

After this, instead of lessons with Mrs. Langtry, I have an American tutor for five weeks and am then enrolled in a private American school until the next March – 1921.

The Major is assigned temporarily to the Presidio in San Francisco, headquarters of the Ninth Corps area, U. S. Army. His transfer requires the passport picture of 1921 which permits the four of us to enter the United States.

Enough of those memories. I am in the U.S.S.R.

Customs! I hoist my one suitcase up on the long counter and open one side. The heavy-set, jovial inspector looks at it casually. I am sure there are no contraband books, magazines or newspapers. I point out three feather-down vests, two blue and one green, for my three sisters.

"Very nice," he says as he motions to close the case and moves to the next person in line. No interest in the Levis for my grand-nephew or the postcards from my U.S. city and the color snapshots of my modest house.

The currency exchange bureau is my final stop. I hand the cashier one hundred dollars; she gives me seventy-five rubles, papers of all colors denoting denominations from one to twenty.

"Don't lose this receipt. It must be shown when you leave the country." I stow it safely in my wallet. "How do I get to Khabarovsk?"

"By going to another airport, Domodedovo."

CHAPTER 4

Intourist – the welcome sign in English and Russian takes the stress off the previous stops. Inside the office, one of six women puts aside her knitting as I approach. "How can I help you?" she asks in accented English. When I answer, "Domodedovo," she points to an exit. "Just stand in line for a taxi. The ride takes about an hour and will cost near ten rubles because you are alone."

My taxi is a Volga, the Rolls Royce of Russian taxis. It has a black and white checkerboard design on the sides with a T in the middle. "What is your name?" I ask the driver. His answer sounds like "Tomdov." His English is as limited as my Russian is, but I get across the idea that I was born in Russia and had never been to Moscow. Good rapport is established.

As we leave the airport, he says with pride, "The largest in the world." A ten-foot high wall of concrete blocks surrounds the airport; a few openings are covered by wire. To reach Domodedovo, we must drive through the center of Moscow.

"Can we drive through the Kremlin?"

"No permit on license," he answers, "but we can drive outside it."

The gates of the Kremlin are at eye level; buildings are not elevated as viewed in the pictures I had seen.

From the taxi window, some nineteenth-century or older buildings in pastel colors, pale blue, pink, soft green and yellow; the often-pictured onion-shaped domes of the cathedrals with geometric designs. What talent! In contrast are the commercial buildings with signs in Cyrillic, of course, that I cannot decipher. The face of President Kosygin decorates many large spaces. Stopped in a traffic jam, I note the majority of delivery trucks have the look of the military – olive-drab and shaped to carry troops, not goods.

At Red Square, with its vast space, lines are already forming to view Lenin's body in his mausoleum. How many know that Petrograd, not Moscow, was the capital before 1918?

The years fall away. I am eight years old. Outside on the dirt road, people are shouting, "Revolution in Petrograd." The news, from the telegraph office, is relayed from person-to-person because few can read. Wild exuberance! Everyone is waving a red cloth or flag. I find a red rag and join the crowd.

In no time, the militia-policeman on his corner becomes a bystander. He no longer scares me with, "Get your mutt out of the way or I'll cut him in half." How dare he call my dear Neptune a mutt with his loving eyes! But I could not help envying this bully his uniform: the crisscross belt over one shoulder supporting a fearful saber, and over the other shoulder, a revolver hanging in its holster.

At home, the revolution is often discussed at the main meal of the day as nine of us sit around the rectangular table built by my father. I do not understand the nuances of the arguments flowing back and forth. But I sense temperatures rising as my parents take the side of the regime of Czar Nicholas II and the three oldest children – two brothers and a sister – vehemently defend their belief for change in line with those of other students at the Khabarovsk Engineering Institute and the teachers college.

If a neighbor interrupts the heated discussion, there is no inkling that we are not a united family. The visit has taken the steam out of the noisy fracas for the present. Subdued, the family drifts off to bed.

Although my father has minor complaints about the czar, my mother voices her complete loyalty. Violence is not in their thinking. And anyway, the center of agitation is almost 5500 miles in Petrograd.

However, suddenly the reality of the revolution is brought home to us. My brothers drop a bomb! They are joining the partisans, known as Bolsheviks. At 14, Mihail, called Misha, claims that he is 18 so that he can join his twenty-year-old brother, Ivan.

Shortly after this, Ivan asks if I would like to see "his" train, commandeered by the revolutionaries. Once inside a first-class compartment, he says, "Go under the settee, Shura, and pick me out two guns." He knows my interest. Holy smoke! What a sight! Guns of all kinds, maybe three dozen: big and little, old and new, nickel-plated, some automatics, some in little leather holsters to fit the palm of the hand. Ivan chooses two revolvers and puts one in each pant-pocket. Already a hero in my eyes, he walks home with me.

Then the rumor circulates that an armed column of the czar's crack troops, the Cossacks, is coming. This professional force of White Russians is more than the revolutionaries are prepared to confront. At the prospect of moving, the partisans become a boisterous mob and start shooting haphazardly – like playing a game of cowboys and Indians but with real ammunition. The next morning, Ivan's train has disappeared.

In its place, an unusual sight on the embankment opposite my house. From behind the trees come three horses, then six, then eight, then twenty, fifty, then one hundred men on horses; I lose count. The officer in front swings his saber and shouts, "Sing, you bastards, sing!" Then the troops in elegant uniforms break into song. The Cossacks on horseback, singing as they ride three abreast along the railroad bed, are magnificent and truly unforgettable.

As a prelude to this show, a General Kalmikov has stopped his train a few miles out of the city. With men and horses unloaded, he rides to the station. Khabarovsk is his without a shot.

But worse is coming! A green box car has been placed on a siding within sight of my house. Each day men and women are escorted to it. The next day, out of my sight down the tracks, the same people are forced inside at the end of a rifle butt. My mother weeps and prays as she watches neighbors and friends, judged traitors without a trial, walking to their deaths by firing squads It is common knowledge.

In spite of Kalmikov's occupation, the revolutionary flame burns brightly underground. For example, our yard is used as a gun-drop for guns smuggled to the partisans in the woods outside the city. The hiding place is under a work table, like a picnic table. On its cross-brace lies a military rifle wrapped in a burlap bag. At dusk, I sometimes see a teenage boy take away the carefully wrapped bundle, and head for the shadowy hideout in the hills, far from the railroad station and city lights. My relieved mother sighs. "Thank goodness, that gun is gone." Until the next gun is hidden, her fears and feelings of guilt leave her.

Eventually, General Kalmikov steams off for Vladivostok in a commandeered train with his Cossacks and horses. History has branded him a butcher.

My brothers return home.

However, no sooner do the Cossacks leave than the Japanese soldiers arrive. Their clothing indicates they are prepared to stay for the Siberian winter: fur parkas and hob-nailed shoes with puttees wrapped around their legs. My friends and I stare as they stand immobile like stocky statues on guarded spots. We sneak around them silently in the snow, eyeing their leather ammunition-belts and rifles with fixed bayonets. We listen hopefully, but often in vain, to hear their odd speech.

There comes a day when the Japanese hold center stage. Mama says, "Shura, we are going to the Square. It is the Emperor's birthday." To me, the emperor and the czar are not real people. I can not imagine either one having a birthday. When we arrive at the central Khabarovsk Square, I see horses standing in perfect formation with a Japanese soldier on each one. Never a movement of horses or men when four three-inch field guns are fired, regulated by a stopwatch in the hand of an official. As the smoke clears, Mama assures me and herself, "Those are blank shells, you know."

My reveries end.

The hour's ride to Domodedovo is almost over. The meter has been clicking – diddle, diddle, diddle. As we continue passing apartment houses, all six to sixteen stories high and tapering at the top, I recall the publicized architecture of the Stalin era. There is much new construction; old wooden houses are being demolished. Lost is the garden, a spot of ground loved and nurtured by Russians for centuries. But the view changes to a gently, rolling landscape along the four-lane highway – trees, trees and more trees – maples, birches, evergreens and other varieties. Many have been symmetrically planted since World War II and are now thirty or forty feet high. Frequent deer crossings pick up the language of pictures, the same the world over.

At last we arrive at Domodedovo. Tomdov seems pleased when I wave aside his return of change from the ten ruble note for the nine-and-twenty-kopeks ride. No tips are the custom.

CHAPTER 5

Domodedovo - the main waiting room. I am not prepared for a combination of Grand Central Station and the New York City subway rush-hour rolled into one. This huge area is packed with people sitting on suitcases, munching bread and fruit, lined up at snack bars waiting for service from women in white caps and lined up at endless ticket windows. Even if Soviet citizens cannot leave the country, they are certainly taking advantage of its far-flung boundaries and the low-cost fares.

In the hubbub, I find a ticket window with only twelve in line.

"You must go to Intourist." I spot the Intourist sign and enter this harbor of refuge in an uncharted sea. Relative peace! I flop onto a sectional couch next to a potted plant and an easy chair. What can I do during my eight-hours before the final leg of my flight to Khabarovsk?

The Beryoska shop has my attention. Here only foreign currency is accepted. On display are beautiful handicrafts: Pelah painted boxes of shellacked wood-paper combination; eight hand-painted dolls, in bright red, yellow and green, graduated in size to be nested together; glowing amber necklaces with matching earrings, hand-embroidered linens and blouses; painted wooden spoons – everything beyond reach of the individuals in the chaotic, crowded waiting room.

To pass the time, I unfold a letter translated from Russian to English to show Tonya. She may have written it for my parents:

Khabarovsk
Maritime Province
27 January 1922

Dear Mr. and Mrs. Langtry:

We have received your letter, informing us of the fate of our son for which we send our sincere thanks. It was not possible to answer on account of certain events which have happened here in the Far East. At the present time, when railroad communication has been restored, we are taking advantage thereof to send you a letter in the hope that you will receive it.

We are very glad that our son found you, as his remaining with the soldiers of the American Army made us very uneasy because soldiers in general cannot be considered good companions for children. Shura (Alek), being brought up in such surroundings might go the wrong way (in a figurative sense). Therefore, you can understand our gratitude to you from the moment when we learned that he had found such a good family as yours.

I consider it unnecessary to inform you of the following mistake of your American consul in Vladivostok. That our son went to America with our permission. No! and a thousand times No! . . . In view of the unfortunate situation which is recurring in the Far East at the present time, we cannot afford to bring Shura (Alek) home as yet; . . Not now, but as soon as the present situation . . . is entirely settled, we hope to see Alek again in his own home. In another letter, you asked to be informed how old Shura is. He was thirteen years old on 5th January 1922. . . . We conclude with the best wishes for you and your family, hoping for a speedy answer, and with gratitude on account of our son.

Names typed by translator – P.I. and A. P. Struchkoff

Another letter was enclosed for me, beginning "Dear Shura."

We are all safe and sound and wish you to be the same. We have two cows, several geese, 15 hens, and we have a nice garden. In the orchard grow plums, renet-apples, strawberries. . . . You write that you have forgotten our names. {The writer gives the names of Alek's sisters and their school status.} We send you many kisses. Papa, Mama, Vania {Ivan}, Motia, Misha, Tonia, Valia and Natenka. We remain your parents, brothers and sisters.

"Struchkoff" was typed at the bottom of this translated letter, the original of which was probably written by Mikhail. {Transliteration of the Cyrillic alphabet varies for certain letters.}

About twenty-five passengers have joined me in the lounge. I think about the controversy over my guardianship when I was eleven. The letters regarding it are safe at home. Let us imagine we are reading them there.

On June 13, 1921 my new father addressed "Captain Richardson, USN, c/o *USS Albany*, Manila, P.I." about a letter received from my mother, addressed to the American Consul in Vladivostok. Lacking diplomatic relations, the United States and Russia find communication complicated.

.The major is now demoted to captain on U.S. soil per customary army procedure in 1921. Also he is put on the defensive in explaining his role in bringing me to the U.S. Meanwhile, he has been assigned to Fort Douglas, Utah.

Two letters finalize the situation. One, dated 14 September 1922, from my mother sent through the Special Delegation of the Far Eastern Republic to the United States of America in D.C.:

"In view of the fact that the boy was taken from home without the consent of the parents, Citizen Struchkova wishes that her son be returned at the expense of Captain Langtry. . . and that conditions on which he may be returned home be determined."

The other from Captain Langtry is a letter that ends a long period of misunderstanding. Dated November 25. 1922, it reads:

"In view of the fact that I did not take the boy out of Siberia and am giving him an education and excellent home, I decline to pay any expense incident to his return to Siberia."

A stalemate!

CHAPTER 6

Still time to kill as I wait for my flight to Khabarovsk. Roaming around the lounge, I hear English spoken by a group of men in a corner. .

Soon I am in conversation with David. He is with correspondents for Western newspapers -- Canadian, West German, French, British and American. He is British.

"What brings you here?" he asks. "You are traveling alone?"

After telling him my purpose and a few details, he says, "I have never talked to a Russian who speaks English with almost no accent and fluently, at that. I'm curious."

"It's a long story. Where shall I begin?"

"I'd really like to know about your earliest years, as you remember them," he answers.

So I begin back in 1914. My first moving day!

Papa has just finished building our four-room wooden house overlooking the Trans-Siberian Railroad. On the morning of that special day, he has roped our belongings – table, beds, bedding and chairs, pots and pans – to a high-sided wagon with a droopy nag in waiting, outside my first home that has faded from memory.

'Shura,' says Papa, "climb up so you won't get lost on the way. I clamber to the top of the pile of household goods. The rest of the family walk behind. What a view! But what potholes in the dirt road! Suddenly I feel the top-heavy load start to shift. Sliding, sliding, falling! Panic-stricken, I scream. With a bone-breaking lurch, I am on the ground looking at the underside of the wagon. The blessed horse has chosen a muddy ditch for my downfall.

In the little house for nine people, the kitchen is the most vivid memory. It is dwarfed by the wood-burning stove which reaches to the ceiling. With the oven, it is used for heating the house, cooking and baking, drying wet coats, pants and mittens in winter. and even incubating eggs during that long, cold season. An open space above it is large enough to hold and warm me in winter but first the bugs have to be swept out. And the space is often a place of banishment to remind me of my bad behavior.

Two of the four rooms are used for sleeping, not enough for parents and seven children, so Valya, four years younger, and I shift from place to place on the floor of the large dining-living room. A soft sheepskin rug is ideal on the floor of railroad ties left over from nearby railroad construction, and a heavy coat of sheepskin is the blanket.

A favorite hideaway is an unfinished space under the peaked roof.

After climbing an outside, wooden ladder, I manage to open the makeshift door with no knob and no hinges. An exciting adventure for a kid as winter winds howl through the timber chinks with icy gusts. Up high, I view endless haystacks beyond our vegetable garden.

Because the railroad is so close, there is always entertainment. The daily – or was it weekly? - pachtova, or mail-passenger train, blows its whistle far away so the townspeople can line up to wave. And the toot of the kerosene car is the signal to rush home and alert the family so one can be first in the long line with an empty drum to be refilled with the vital kerosene.

Another kind of entertainment: I often visit the track-walker who lives nearby. When he says, 'Have you come to help me today?' I follow him and try to keep up as he bangs the track-spikes with a heavy hammer. The ringing sound is intriguing even if I am too small to handle the hammer.

And then there is the mystery of the four-wheel hand carts being pushed on the tracks. Do the layers of straw cover the victim of a train accident or the victim of a stabbing from a vodka imbiber?

All the real activities are better than today's TV.

'I'd like to hear about your family that you left fifty-seven years ago,' says David.

Therefore, I give him some highlights of how they acted. I have no pictures of them, and I can't remember how they looked.

In retrospect, my father, like most Russians, had a weakness for vodka, but it did not affect the family relationship, except perhaps economically. He was a man who knew what was right and tried to instill that belief into his children.

To illustrate, my brother, Mikhail, learns a lesson of fairness and tolerance when he returns home after buying a sack of grain for our pigs. But instead of slinging it over his shoulder to carry it, he has hired a Chinese to do it for him. The two fellows arrive at our door. My father pays the Chinese. But then he goes into a rage at Mikhail with curses and a stick. 'Stop! Stop!' yells the Chinese, trying to return the money. 'No, no! You earned that,' says Papa, as he makes a vain attempt to whack Mikhail, too strong for him to throttle. My brother does not want to lose face and hollers as if killed. He knows better than to challenge my father's authority.

Another episode shows an inconsistent side of Papa. After one of my episodes of misbehavior, he is chasing me through mud and thickets When he catches me about a mile from our house, he gives me a whipping, a weak one because he is exhausted from running after me. At home, he lays his head on the table to catch his breath. Shortly, overcome with remorse, he puts a 10-kopek in my hand. All is forgiven.

My father was away much of the time, often working at a fish plant on the Kamchatka peninsula, a long boat-trip from home. I remember the monthly routine to get his pay. Mama would say, 'Shura, today you get Papa's money from the paymaster.' His house is an hour's walk. One time when I arrive, he is sitting, big and fat, in a comfortable armchair, picking sunflower seeds from a bowl, one by one. 'Sit down, Alek, and have some seeds.' They are my favorite fast food. As we both munch seeds together, spitting the husks on the floor, slowly his eyelids droop and so do mine. When I wake up, he is still sitting in the same position, now and then reaching for a seed. After giving me Papa's monthly rubles, he complains as usual about poor fishing and little money. I head for home. Not stopping anywhere, I put the crumpled, damp papers from my hot, tight fist into Mama's welcoming hands. She smiles lovingly, saying, 'Shura, you are a good boy.' I feel important.

When Papa arrives for the holidays, it is time to celebrate: little glowing candles on a real tree, Japanese tangerines and gifts. One Christmas when I am six or seven, I receive a wonderful coat, an exact copy of one worn by the czar's famous Cossacks. It has wooden buttons on each side with a gold belt. I wear it to shreds.

Although we had a garden and even had a pig slaughtered from time to time for meat during winter, staples were purchased at a grocery run by Chinese. My mother often needed me to carry packages and sometimes I was asked to buy a few items. One day when I laid out my purchases on the table at home, Mama says, 'Where is the sugar?' I start to cry with visions of a spanking. However, my mother takes off her apron, takes my hand and off we go to the store, a half-hour's walk. At the store, she says, 'You took money from my boy for sugar, but didn't give him any.'

'Sure I gave him sugar. He must have lost it,' says the Chinese clerk. Sugar was rationed, unknown to me, so the missing item had special significance.

The discussion continues but my mother never budges from her stand. At last the Chinese gives in. I feel much taller after Mother has taken my side with such firmness.

My mother provided the influence of her religion, the Russian orthodox. She had an icon in her bedroom and after supper, she would say, 'It is time for your prayers, Shura.' I obediently knelt in front of the icon, not really knowing what it was all about nor being told how to pray or for what to pray.

As I look back, my brothers and their friends seemed to elevate my humble house to an unusual plane of intellect. Ivan and Misha always brought books home and often their friends from the Institute came with them.

While their talk is beyond my understanding, I look with envy at Ivan's dark green trousers with a strap at the instep and his multi-pocket jacket – both give him an elegant air that makes me proud of him.

Ivan gives the house a lift in a practical way when he uses his engineering knowledge to lay a walk of railroad ties from the house to the railroad embankment – about 100 feet. A blessing to walk on wood instead of through mud!

Mikhail, seven years older than I, and more impulsive than Ivan, was always up to something exciting. I remember the day he decided to go hunting for rabbits close to home.

'My gunpowder is too wet to load into my shotgun,' he says to Mama. 'How long has the oven been cooling?'

'The fire died long ago,' is her answer.

Therefore, Mikhail puts an open can of powder about six inches inside the oven door, saying. 'I'll take it out in a few minutes.'

Meanwhile, I am chopping kindling wood outside with Ivan and Mikhail standing near me. Suddenly, I look up. Wow! A sheet of blue flame, the width of the open door, flashes past my brothers. I drop my ax and run into the house. Mother is coming out of her bedroom, unaware of the scary happening. And the netting is gone from her flour sieve as it hangs on the wall.

My oldest sister, Motya. steps into marriage when I am eight after her graduation from the teachers college. She and her husband, who fascinated me with his glasses of thick lenses, leave for a home-school assignment at a remote forest spot. He later reported, 'I was scared to death of being held up, but was ready with my pen knife in case someone tried to rob me.'

The lounge clock shows our wait is no longer eight hours. It is getting dark, and the number in the lounge has increased to about one hundred.

CHAPTER 7

"Your plane will be ready to board in a few minutes," the uniformed attendant tells me. With no seats assigned, I must line up now to avoid the last-minute scramble. I take a seat on the aisle.

The plane lifts off; a steep ascent. Red apples come rolling down the aisle from cartons in a lavatory; the passengers roll them back. The ice is broken; laughter substitutes for language. Hard candies are passed in the non-pressurized cabin of the Ilusha 62 as we start to fly over 5000 miles through seven time-zones.

Soon two stewardesses in light-blue uniforms are wheeling our dinners on a cart down the aisle. A small tray holds the traditional Russian appetizer of black and red caviar on top of buttered bread. The rest of the meal is a tasty steak with potatoes, salad, pickle, cheese, a sweet cake and tea. No vodka is ever offered during the journey, but from time to time lemonade or soda water.

As we fly at about 15,000 feet, I know the Trans-Siberian Railroad is somewhere below us. I also know a portion of that famous railroad, the longest in the world, because it changed my life.

In the fall of 1918, rumors at home and on the street are about the possible arrival of "Americanski" soldiers. Then THE DAY!

*****

At this time, the attention of the world was focused on the First World War. In 1918, the United States was fighting with its allies, Britain, France, Italy and Japan. Because Russia was in the throes of a revolution and civil war, the Soviet government negotiated to free itself from the entanglement with the Allies. Meanwhile, they put pressure on the U.S. President, Woodrow Wilson, to send troops to open an eastern front in Russia against Germany and in support of 40,000 Czeck soldiers, formerly a unit of the Russian Army. They were reported to be headed for Vladivostok. It was thought the move, quite controversial, would expedite an end to the war. However, although the Armistice was signed on November 11, 1918, a couple of months after the troops arrived in Siberia, they stayed for eighteen months. "In Siberia, it marked the first serious interference in an Asian land war," according to Richard O'Connor, writing "Yanks in Siberia," which appeared in *American Heritage* for August 1974.

We return to Alec, the eye-witness.

*****

From the front window of my house, I see a freight train standing on a siding. Soldiers in khaki uniforms are unloading a box car; I have never seen one like it; a big shield is painted on it with red and white stripes topped by white stars on a blue background.

I go outside for a better look.

They are piling wooden boxes, crates, and barrels in rows beside the tracks. Because there is no warehouse, what next? They will be guarded each day at sunset by soldiers with fixed bayonets marching back and forth.

The khaki uniforms are different from the familiar ones of the Russian and Japanese soldiers. First, these soldiers look neater because their shirttails are tucked inside their trousers. Then an odd curlicue on the upper left sleeve {S}; nothing like it in the Russian alphabet.

I soon discover the mobile field kitchen in back of the supply train. Jim, the harassed cook, is patient for a long time with my curiosity about the thousands of cans . But one day he gives in with a can from his huge supply. 'Take this, kid, and get out.'

I take it and crawl under the raised platform used for outdoor boxing matches. I pry open the can with my trusty jackknife, With the thunder of stomping feet, whistles and cheers, I gorge on the most luscious cherries of my life. Later, I recognized the name, Tea Garden.

Meanwhile, under my constant supervision, the boxes and barrels are unpacked containing unusual tools and shiny nails; timbers arrive from the local sawmill on wagons drawn by strange looking horses – I never heard of mules – and a new building rises close to home.

The activities of the soldiers change my life. Instead of waiting for the passing of the mail-passenger train and watching the Japanese soldiers here and there, I watch the Americans as often as possible – on the way to school, on the way home, -- morning, noon and night, if possible. School and its lessons are not important to me.

But they are **very** important to my parents. No longer am I at the railroad school with its relative freedom – a kind of pre-school and kindergarten. I now attend the "gimnasia," or elementary school, where I have a report card, like a notebook, with marks for studies on one side and marks for conduct on the other. It is taken home every week to show my parents. My conduct marks never please them. They ask, "Why can't you do well like your brothers and sisters?" Why do they not understand that what goes on outside the window is more interesting than inside?

My parents think punishment, such as whipping or kneeling on rice in a corner, will help my conduct at home or at school. (They never heard of psychology of any kind.) I remember when I washed the kitchen floor of railroad ties with kerosene, and the time I broke a glass chimney for the kerosene lamp that slipped from my hands when washing it in precious, hot soapy water. I thought I was being helpful but Mama didn't see it that way.

Moreover, while some pupils arrive at school in horse-drawn sleighs, I trudge about two miles on foot. If it is winter and I walk through a puddle with a hole in my boot, I will soon be standing on an icicle. But a friendly cobbler on the way to school always comes to my rescue. "Take off your boot, Alek," he says as I enter his cubby hole. In a second, it is returned with the hole stitched, not patched, on his heavy machine. No money – only thanks. I am off to school with a dry foot.

Three problems constantly disturb my 10-year-old mind: my poor marks at school, my inability to please my parents and lack of money. A solution might be possible!

Therefore, after a particularly poor report card and foreseeing either harsh words or a whipping, I meander the streets of Khabarovsk, trying to straighten out my muddled thoughts. Before I know it, I am at a small, red building. It is warm inside on a dreary, cold afternoon. With pipes and valves all around, I recognize it as the city water-pumping station. The unknown man in charge says, "Sleep here, if you like." I go to sleep on the floor in my sheepskin coat, no questions asked.

At first light, a farm wagon holding a water tank stops at the window with a long pipe protrudng from it. The driver, an American soldier, comes inside until the tank is filled. He drives away, but returns several times for more water. On the final trip, he looks at me and invites me, with gestures, for a ride. "Da. da," is my thrilled positive answer. It is my first and most fateful ride in a wagon pulled by mules.

Away we go to a building now known as the American hospital. It is surrounded by trees close to the railroad and about a half-mile from my house. A brick building, formerly used by czarist troops, it has always been off-limits to townspeople.

The driver takes me inside. Someone puts a plate of stew in my lap, then a chocolate bar and chewing gum.

This hospital stop is supposed to be a short one while the tank is drained. Then what? Home, of course.

"Where do you live?" asks an interpreter.

"My parents are dead," I lie in Russian. "I live at the orphanage." I had heard that there was one in the city.

The young soldiers know they must check my story. Therefore, two of them and the interpreter take me in a wagon to the city orphanage. I see it for the first time. The old gatekeeper is sitting outside an iron gate. I am shaking with fright.

"Have you seen this boy before?" inquires the interpreter.

"Yes, I believe so, but we have so many boys, it is hard to keep track of them when they run away." I understand correctly that the soldiers' smiles mean, "You can stay with us."

The gatekeeper never protests their decision to drive away with me. Uniforms may have always intimidated him and American ones were no different than czarist ones in his mind.

In relief that my lie is confirmed as the truth, I break into tears. My new friends misinterpret them as a sign of fear at the prospect of returning to the orphanage. They are convinced I am telling the truth. For them and for me, there seems no barrier to prevent me from staying at the American hospital. The men welcome me as an unexpected form of entertainment.

I lose count of the days, often spent poking my nose into areas limited to the medical staff. But I never heard any of them say, "Get out of here, Alek," nor did I ever hear them speak to my mentors of their decision to keep me – a fake orphan only to myself.

One day I spy my mother from my sleeping quarters in the squad room at the rear of the hospital. She is outside the camp boundary, looking for me. I watch her in silence. I think my mother's life will be easier without my mouth to feed. As an immature, starry-eyed kid of ten, I make a decision too momentous for my years, not thinking of her heartache. I miss my family but the attention and new activities of my present life outweigh my understanding of their feelings.

However, after several weeks, this paradise comes to an end. Mikhail finds me. "What are you doing here? We've been looking everywhere but never thought of asking or looking for you here."

To the astonishment of my family, I arrive home in an army wagon accompanied by three soldiers, an interpreter and a footlocker of gifts – chewing gum, candy and army clothing that can only be imagined. And I proudly wear my prized

U.S. Army uniform that Jim, the cook and one of my mentors, has put together with parts of a worn-out uniform.

With cheerful goodbyes and an invitation to visit the medical unit again, these American soldiers feed my dreams. In spite of extra attention and little punishment at home, I am satisfied for only a few weeks.

Another crisis! I walk the short distance to the embankment of the Trans-Siberian Railroad and climb the wooden steps to the tracks. After the short walk to the station, I hop on the first train that stops. As the conductor looks down at me in my shabby, cut-down uniform, he accepts as a ticket my words, "Traveling with American soldiers." It is the first of many journeys, by train or by foot.

During daylight, an American flag flying near the tracks signals an American camp.

Leaving my town on the main line in late afternoon, I junp off at the next station, Red River, with a group of American soldiers. They are waiting for a train to take them along a spur to their encampment somewhere in the woods. When their freight train arrives, they jump aboard and I am left alone at the station. I will not be so lonely if I start walking along the tracks in the same direction as the freight. In the twilight, snow is falling and the tracks stretch to infinity. I kick myself for not taking the train with the soldiers. Suddenly it is dark; big flakes of snow are floating down. An occasional plop startles me as an evergreen branch lets go of its heavy load of the white stuff. The landscape is eerie in the faint light from an opaque moon. Then my heart jumps with fright. A peculiar metallic, gurgling sound comes from behind me, then closer. Finally, I can see a man's outline. He stops to size me up; just a kid. I am scared. When he comes abreast of me with a five-gallon drum on his back, I see he is Chinese. With every step he takes in the snowy stillness, the liquid in his can sloshes loudly. We walk side by side for an hour or more along the tracks without ever exchanging a word. Our long walk ends when he veers off into the cover of the surrounding dark woods.

I plod along the tracks still visible under the light snow-covering. I discover that they are not laid uniformly. It is always one long step, then a short one, endlessly. Not a glimmer of light appears down the tracks. But then they curve. Through the trees far away, I see a light. My spirits lift. I see an American flag. I shed freezing tears of relief.. It is the first camp outside the boundaries of my home city. Remembering my friend, Jim, the mess sergeant, I find his counterpart, the most important person for me. With my makeshift uniform, it is easy to convince him that I am traveling to visit relatives but am living with the medical unit in Khabarovsk. He gives me a meal. Never, I recall, am I ever refused food at an army camp. Never!

Next morning when I am finishing breakfast after occupying an empty cot, a soldier asks, "Where are you going now?"

"Spaask," I answer, a well-known town south of my city.

"There is no train to Spaask."

I decide to wait at the nearby railroad stop for any train going south. I swing on the back platform of the first one that comes; the last car is green. The train starts; the clickity-clack of the wheels lulls me. A door opens, an arm yanks me into a Japanese armored car. I have forgotten that the armored car of the Japanese is green; the American is brown. The excited gibberish between the puzzled soldiers is surely asking why this kid is wearing an American uniform of sorts. At the next station, I am dragged to the platform. As my fate is being discussed by the Japanese soldiers, I see an American box car inching in sight. With new-found strength, I jerk my hand from my captor's grasp and catch a rung on the ladder of the familiar train. I am welcomed by old friends who recognize the worn uniform. Once again I am riding south.

As trains carry me along for a week or so that seems longer, I oversleep on a train headed for Nikolayevsk and wake up in a railroad yard; – tracks stretch out of sight. I am certainly in Vladivostok. A passenger train is preparing to move. Where else but north toward Khabarovsk? I hop on confidently; my army coat keeps me warm and my wool hat is a soft pillow.

When I wake up this time, I see smokestacks on top of factories. Off the train, I hear the word "Harbin." The name of this large city in China is somewhat familiar. I stroll to a small park where a Chinese woman shares her lunch with me – sausage, boiled egg and bread. She bemoans her son, lost in Russia.

Finally, I return to Vladivostok and haphazardly continue my journeys with the red, white and blue flag as my signal to stop.

CHAPTER 8

An hour more of flying! On this long journey, I have relived in memory much of my life, especially my first years. And my last days in Russia stand out with unusual clarity.

I remember how, finally, I come to the small station of Sviagino, a long ride south of Khabarovsk. Here is my turning point!

Rows of tents stretch farther than I can see in the clearing of woods.. Snow is already on the ground. Winter weather has caught up with the soldiers before the barracks is built. Heroic pioneers!

One of them finds a sleeping place for me in an eight-man tent. My cot is of canvas with a wood frame and metal bindings on the cross-supports. The mattress is a big pillowcase filled with straw, covered by a wool blanket with another to cover me. At reveille, a soldier kicks my cot. "Get up, kid." It is his cot and time for me to move. He wears two pairs of long-johns under three layers of clothing.

Although I receive no formal invitation to stay in this camp, my presence is accepted.

I soon learn that the encampment is that of Company G, 27th Infantry, American

Expeditionary Force (Siberia); and that the soldiers have come from a warm climate, the Philippine Islands.

(According to army rosters that confirm the names of the men I knew, the approximate dates I spent in this camp were from September 1919 to February 1920. At age ten, it had seemed much longer.)

With more than 230 men in the Company, a barracks takes shape shortly. Its construction is no problem with wood waiting to be cut, a sawmill close by and soldiers with many talents.

But what really holds my attention is the way the men transform a coal car into an armored car. Inside the wood lining is a space about a foot-and-a half wide filled with sand; built-in bunks for twelve men. and machine guns poke out of a cupola on top. As I look at it, I remember my narrow escape from the green armored car manned by the Japanese soldiers.

Two soldiers give me special attention: Private Scott {who has already been mentioned} and First Sergeant Edward McGuire.

These soldiers teach me, with much patience, the rules that I must memorize which will allow me to camp of I leave the boundaries. The words become second nature and I am learning a little English.

‘Halt! Who goes there?’ asks the guard.

‘Friend,’ I answer immediately.

‘Advance, Friend, and be recognized.’ I walk slowly toward him.

‘Halt!’ he repeats.

And I often follow a soldier for no good reason, but only so far; never am I allowed to enter any private house in the village.

At night, the reluctant footsteps of the corporal of the guard crunch through the snow in the bitter cold as he comes from the guard house. The kerosene lamp lighting his way lets him see I am the kid-mascot.

No electric light shines on the individual who has to wait at the gate to be recognized. Sometimes a girl friend from the village waits with the soldier for a good-night kiss. Perhaps he’s carrying a bottle of contraband vodka.

Speaking of vodka, I recall one night when asleep in the warm bake shop, my regular place, where the morning bread is baking. Heavy thumps on the side of the building wake me; the double-pane window shatters. Standing inside the window is one of the bakers holding his loaded Springfield rifle. Outside several soldiers are trying to subdue a buddy. The baker puts down his gun and adds only his fisticuffs to the noisy melee.

The next day at the spot of the fracas, I find a pair of gloves on the frozen snow-covered ground. I put them on – finders, keepers.. A few days later, a soldier stops me.

"Hey, kid! Aren't those the gloves I dropped when I had the fight?" My hands are cold again as I return them with chagrin. My clear conscience compensates for my frozen fingers.

`No one has time to answer my questions when hectic activity is the order of the day. On a night of numbing cold, I hear the bugler sounding a haunting strain that I never forgot, "Recall." The trumpet sounds echo for miles in the Siberian silent dark. The footsteps of the soldiers are muffled by the snow as they return to camp after farewells to Russian friends, men and women, in the village. 'Til we meet again? Never!

We are "breaking" camp.

The box cars, loaded with soldiers and equipment, leave at midnight for Vladivostok, the seaport. I am with a sergeant who, I am told, has married a Russian woman. She cooks in the box car for him, other soldiers and myself. . How I wish I could remember the food and the stove!

At Vladivostok, the train is shunted to the dockyard area not far from a towering army transport ship, *Great Northern.*

Up to now, it hadn't seemed that my family was far away. I had thought of sending some token winnings from small-bit card games, but my bounty dribbled away. However, my parents, brothers and sisters, remained fixed in my mind. And I always felt I could see them when I wished.

The troops are boarding the ship. And I am intent on boarding too. But how?

I look up and see soldiers, nurses, army officers and ship officers leaning over the promenade deck railing. I feel sure that someone up there will chase me away if they see me walking up the gangway with the troops. So I wait until no soldiers, nurses, army officers and ship officers are looking over the railing. Then I, in my little army uniform, line up between two soldiers. We walk up the gangway to the boarding doors. As each man enters through the low doorway, his name is called out by a corporal, confirming the soldier's presence and right to be on board.

My companions' turn comes. A hand falls on my shoulder. The two boarding corporals hesitate; they look at each other over my head; then a slight push. I am in!

Like a squirrel with a nut, I quickly go below to look for a safe hiding place. I burrow into a top bunk behind some barracks bags hung there. Since the ship is not full, there is extra space. I hide until the engine noises change and I figure the ship is far from the pier. For the next seven days, Private Scott gets in line for his food, eats, washes his kit, and then gets in line again for my meal which he brings to my hiding place.

It is time to come back to the present as I hear the welcome announcement of imminent arrival at my destination over the loudspeaker.

PART II

THE BRIDGE IS REPAIRED

CHAPTER 9

Khabarovsk airport! A flight of seven and a half hours from Moscow – what an immense country!

As I walk to a street exit through the main building with spectators looking down from a balcony, I hear a voice, "Aleksandr Andreivich." That's me. A handsome, well-built woman is coming toward me with a bunch of flowers. After giving them to me, she gives me a kiss. More kisses and hugs. This must be Tonya. "Nyet, nyet!' {No, no} She pulls me to the front of the building.

Tonya, older and thinner than my greeter, stands with tears in her eyes, lines of care and character on her wrinkled face. The flowers are dropped. More hugging and crying; no one able to speak because of the language barrier. But after fifty-seven years, emotions are too deep for words.

A young man is standing in the background watching this joyful, tearful reunion. I know at once it is Tonya's son, Marik, whom she had mentioned in a letter. He puts an end to a momentary self-conscious silence, "Oh, baggage." He takes the hand of his little son, Sasha, and three of us walk to the revolving carrier. As I find and walk away with my bag, the strident voice of a woman says, "Yip, yip, yip, your tag." I dig it out of a pocket.

Marik drives us in his Russian Fiat, a sickly green, to Tonya's apartment diagonally across from the railroad station which overlooks the central square.

Three flights up to number 11, through a little hallway, we enter a room about 12 x 18 feet. From it, I can see a small bathroom and a kitchen, lighted by a window high up in the wall.

The arrival of Madame Marguarita, a university teacher and our interpreter, solves the communication problem for the present.

What a good time we have as I show colored snapshots of my 1971 International Scout car, my modest two-story wood house and the surrounding land. All photos have been taken with a small Instamatic camera. "We don't have photos like that here," says Marik's wife, who had joined the onlookers.

"Well, we have postcards like that," adds Marik, somewhat on the defensive.

I mention that my house has eight rooms. Tonya asks, "What would I do with those eight rooms? Why do you need so much space?"

After an hour, I unpack. It is time to give Tonya her blue vest and Marik his Levis. Motya will have her green vest later.

They leave and let me have a rest in the one room divided by a curtain.

The next morning, I note the details of the apartment. Tonya has a well-filled bookcase; no television. "I don't like television. Everyone tells me to get a television. I don't want one." However, she has a one-station wall-radio in the kitchen which receives Radio Moscow. Her reading and her friends inform her of world events. A small icon is nestled among some flower pots on the kitchen window.

"How do you think I got my telephone and my refrigerator?" she asks, "You've got to have good connections. Because of my former position,{Russian Red Cross} I have good friends, very good friends." She has had the refrigerator only two years.

Because I cannot converse in Russian, I am happy walking and exploring Khabarovsk.

As I leave for my first tour, Tonya draws my attention to a two-foot space in front of her door – the tenant's responsibility. The door itself is studded with metal spikes and the latest addition to the leatherette covering, a peephole.

Down three flights of dirty, dusty stairs, I note the landings for which I will be grateful on my return. The odors of fish and butchering blend with those of the overloaded garbage containers. Thank God for the fresh air!

I exit at the back of the six-story building which is also the entrance because the first floor is occupied by businesses: a book store, a meat market and a tiny art gallery.

On my way across the street to the railroad station, I see a little wagon with the sign, Kvass, a Russian soft drink. A ring of men, all holding mugs, surround it,. I ask. “Is Kvass sold here?” Only beer is the answer. My first lesson: not all soft-drink wagons sell soft drinks.

All the sights are new! But the square where I had seen the celebration of the Japanese Emperor’s birthday now holds a statue of Erofei Pavlovich Khabarov, the founder of the city. Two wide boulevards on either side give it a a grand air. The four-story, stucci railroad station overlooking the square is a far cry from the red brick building that I recall dimly, a short walk from my house.

To investigate the station, I climb ten steps – yes, I counted them – on a concrete stairway over thirty feet wide with no handrail. As I push through a swinging double door, I see the usual ticket windows, but the service counters are selling whiskey in addition to soft drinks, ice cream, postcards, toys, *Pravda* and *Izvetzia* and, of course, magazines..

Again I hear the whir of a vacuum cleaner, the first had been at the Domededovo airport. This time three men are pushing the big machine with its hose and 200 feet of electric cord. Make way! It wets the area as it moves. Utter confusion! Not only is the dirty floor covered by scores of travelers' feet, but paper bags and bundles tied with string, suitcases of all shapes and sizes, new and battered, and cigarette butts galore. If the vacuum cannot do its job, the debris on the floor will be deeper. And off in a corner is another daily vacuum cleaner, an old woman with a reed broom.

Light floods the waiting room on this bright afternoon. I count nineteen windows facing the street and the same number facing the Amur River – all with double panes. Each window is about ten by twenty feet at least. Some cracks have been repaired.

The double-pane windows remind me how the small double-pane one in my childhood home kept the winter chill out; and the snow sparkling in the sun on many days belied the gray-cold picture associated with the word, Siberia.

Curious and with time on my hands, I walk down to the basement: more waiting room, toilets, storage rooms and more food counters. As in waiting rooms the world over, drunks keep warm and sleep on benches. I witness a small drama.

A policeman wakes a sleeper. "Where is your ticket? Show me your ticket." With the ticket in his hand, "Uh, oh, you missed your train. It left two hours ago. Go up and validate your ticket." Another man who has no ticket, is chased out with the words I've heard used world-wide, but not in Russian, "This is no flophouse."

As I leave the building, I see an overhead pass. A series of steps with wood platforms and a steel railing offer safety as I cross over twelve tracks of the Khabarovsk railroad yard. Purple railway switches glow along the tracks in the twilight. Trains waiting on the sidings read "Vladivostok – Birobidzhan" and "Vladivostok – Blagoveshchensk," black lettering on white paneling.

The next day, Tonya has a suggestion. "How would you like to see the graves of our parents?" Although the question had never occurred to me until that moment, I acquiesce. Therefore, Marik comes with two friends and drives us to a wooded area. The road peters out. We walk through a gate and, by a roundabout path, come to a steel-pipe fence. A photo of my mother under glass on a pole is near her tombstone with her birth and death dates, 1876 and 1963.

Not a word is said. My thoughts are too many and too complex, even if I could communicate in Russian. I bend down with the others to pull the weeds from the mound. A hushing experience! A lilac bush over a wrought-iron cross of the Russian Orthodox church will give a touch of beauty in the spring. The cross on her grave is a symbol of the believer; the graves of the non-believers are marked with metal red stars.

Further, we tramp through another overgrown path to my father's grave with his dates, 1878 to 1943. A poplar tree stands guard. He had committed suicide by hanging.

CHAPTER 10

The telephone rings in Tonya's apartment. Sondra is calling from Kiev, Because my hearing is poor, she says, "Let me talk to Tonya." Sondra tells Tonya in Russian that she will come by plane and send a telegram when on her way. Delivered by a pretty girl, the telegram arrives: leaving for Khabarovsk.

Marik drives Tonya and me to the airport to meet Sondra's plane. No Sondra. No foreigner on the plane; no passport identifies her. Therefore, back to Tonya's. Next day, we meet **four** flights from Moscow – I think there is only one. Still no Sondra.

For two days, impatient and worried, we meet planes. Intourist has no help for us, although the agency keeps track of foreigners for aid in addition to security reasons.

The third day, at four in the morning, the doorbell rings. I open the door. Sondra at last! Hugs and kisses in the dark. I had last seen her in Egypt over a year before..

Here is the long story of her delay, in her own words, a young Russian-speaking American maneuvering communist Russia alone:

First, as I walk into the ladies' room of the Kiev airport, a man with a small boy, says, 'Haven't you gotten mixed up?' I respond in Russian, 'Isn't this the ladies?' Another woman says, 'Yes, it's the ladies.' He leaves hurriedly with the boy, saying, 'Oh, it's I who have gotten mixed up.'

I arrive in Ynukovo airport in Moscow, and take a bus to Domodedovo airport. Mobs of people, mobs, - two long lines for two information bureaus.

Finally a small blue sign, Intourist, in a window. Down steps, foreigners waiting, not too crowded.

'You have to go to the Metropole to get your ticket,' says the Intourist woman in a clean blue uniform.

'I don't have a visa for Moscow.' (I try a ploy; having already been an hour and fifteen minutes on the bus.) This means the same time back to the city, then the Metro {subway}. Why had I not been told of this complication?

'Can't we put her on flight so-and-so?' asks a second Intourist.

'No, we don't have permission from Khabarovsk.'

So, I'm on the bus headed back to the center of Moscow. . . In the Moscow metro. I ask the change-maker for the Metropole hotel. She mumbles . 'Sverdlova' in a loud voice and holds up three fingers. Sverdlov Square at rush hour!

Arriving at the hotel, I am told to go to Hall #3 for transit. . . . Flight for Khabarovsk leaves at 8:47 pm. It is now about 5:15 pm. . . . Now I must send a telegram to Khabarovsk . . . Metropole telegraph office is closed. I'm fighting against time.

Where is the main telegraph office? Gorky Square. I buck the crowds. . . . I scribble on a blue telegraph blank, 'Arrive 11:25 pm.' Two hours and thirty minutes to flight time. I rush out of the building to a pedestrian underpass, then another. I come to the surface and have not crossed any street. Up and down for nothing. I laugh to myself. Rush, rush, huff, huff. . . . By the time I get off the bus, I have a half-hour to spare, but it's too late. I didn't realize that foreign passengers get on the plane direct from the Intourist lounge without lining up in the main waiting room. My plane has left. 'That will be 25 rubles for missing your plane.' But pleading ignorance, I am not charged.

I move to the Intourist lounge and sleep okay on a red couch. Flight #35 non-stop to Khabarovsk finally leaves at 11:15 am. I am the only foreigner from the Intourist lounge on the flight. I am boarded first and seated on the aisle in the back of the first compartment. After the Soviet passengers arrive, the plane is full. . . . I arrive at 11:45 pm Far East time after a smooth, uneventful flight.

I wait with the others an hour and a half for my baggage in a small wooden structure separate from the terminal. 'Yours is at Intourist.' There is a line of about twenty people waiting in line for taxis. The young woman at Intourist lounge, now dark, insists on calling a cab in spite of my protests. I am not used to the special treatment. 'Your relatives have been worried. They have been calling all day but I think they sleep at this time of night.'

After a day of rest, Sondra says to me, "I will go anywhere you want."

"O.K. Let's go down to the old homestead. You know it's not there anymore." This is my second visit to the location as I had gone to the spot with Tonya the previous week.

We cross five or six tracks – no overpass – looking in both directions for trains moving back and forth constantly. The former single track to Vladivostok is now a double one. The 300-foot embankment is no longer the 30-foot one I knew. Close to it is a small sign reading, "Moscow 8524 kilometers."

After surviving more than sixty years, my house had been torn down about ten years before after my nephew, then a teenager, fell through the roof. Only a ten-minute walk past the railroad station, the house had seemed miles from home years ago.

As we walk down a slight incline, Sondra says, "The garden still has a fence and there are the sunflowers with your favorite seeds." Sure enough. I take the head off a flower to keep me supplied with those favorites as we continue our exploration.

Wooden one-family dwellings; tall green grass. Down a muddy path, we pass a man carrying two pails of water from a corner pump; the water sloshes on the ground. He lives in a wooden apartment-house complex. We go to the entrance at the back. His wife comes out, smiling and showing her silver teeth.

"I remember when you left," she says speaking through Sondra. "Your mother cried and cried. She looked everywhere for you. She even went to Vladivostok." (According to Tonya, my mother went to Vladivostok with my photo; she went to the ship and held it up to the soldiers at the gangplank. 'Have you seen this boy?' They shook their heads. No doubt, I was already on the ship. I lived to write this story.)

"Yes," continues the woman with the silver teeth, "things have improved a lot since then. Do you remember how we used to light the houses with those little lamps? They would flicker in the darkness. All around there would be little flickers of light."

By this time, other people have come out of the one-story building. divided into eight apartments. In my day, railroad workers had lived there. The present occupants cannot believe that I have traveled from a mysterious land overseas to see this special spot which they take for granted.

Most of these tenants, with children in the day nursery or so-called creche, appreciate having a plot of ground to work. "We have electricity. But toilets are outhouses and water comes from a well." Free wood is dropped off from the nearby sawmill for the wood-burning stoves. The honey-wagon which comes to clean the outhouses is driven over a two-lane asphalt road instead of over the little dirt back alley by a Chinese that I remember.

Beyond this highway is an old warehouse of the czarist regime, one of twenty, all about 40 by 100 feet. A platform remains outside a barbed wire enclosure where a guard patrolled. All of the buildings are hidden by trees.

The sight of these buildings reminds me of a reference by Tonya that I was born in a wooden house in a Khabarovsk school yard. Might it be traced to the employ of my maternal grandfather for twenty-five years in the czar's military? This privilege, suggested by a Russian friend, might possibly have been granted to the daughter of a faithful soldier as a bonus.

Continuing our walk, I see freshly painted signs marking battle sites: names, dates and number of men killed at the spot. Then we pass an outlet of the river, a swimming hole for my brothers and me. But no longer; filled in and leveled, a health hazard has been removed..

As we amble along the shaded sidewalk to my old schoolhouse, now used by Youth Pioneers, the counterpart of Boy Scouts, we see two boys coming toward us. Son-of-a-gun! One has a twelve-foot python wrapped around his waist like a belt. He holds its head up to give us a good look. Not appreciated. We give the boys a wide berth. No spirit of adventure for snakes. But their cute Siberian husky dog softens the picture.

Our walk ends with a tour of the Institute of Railroad Engineers. We go up the worn marble steps to a cavernous lobby, Although I cannot read the informative pamphlet, Sondra tells me that the Institute is one of a complex that includes thirty scientific-research institutes in addition to eight institutes of higher learning with dormitories for thousands of students and faculty, all founded since 1930. The first technical school, the Institute of Railroad Transport Engineers, was founded in 1939. Whatever institute my brothers were attending in 1917-18 has probably been incorporated in this school. In the year of 1976, it has 8000 students, 500 teachers and nine departments.

An institute official gives us a private tour. In his early forties and soft-spoken, he is tall and too stooped for his age. It is the first day of classes and he takes a half hour out of his busy schedule to show us around.

Most impressive to me are mock booths representing control rooms of various stations on the Trans-Siberian for students to practice switching and traffic controls, switching and circuit models, lots of circuitry, a computer center. I am not qualified to judge the vintage of the latter.

Every aspect of railroading is covered in this institute. Long ago the coal and wood-burning engines of my childhood have been replaced by diesel/electric ones. But the railroad still uses two systems of switching: the old-fashioned one where the trainman gets off the train and throws the switch, and the newer block-signal system in which switches are controlled electronically at a dispatching office miles away.

CHAPTER 11

The word, "dacha," has become a reality. Two visits to Tonya's: one with her by train, and the other by car with Sondra, Machi, his six-year-old son, Sasha, and Tonya.

First, the expedition alone with Tonya. A 30-minute train ride for 15 or 20 kopeks, takes us to the fifth whistle-stop, Khekhitsir, also the name of the low hills along our route, about 12 kilometers south of the city. Off the train, we walk a mile along a dirt road lined with wooden buildings, the size of tool sheds, in tiny plots bordered by wooden fences. These are dachas. Each plot, a fraction of an acre, is through "connections."

It is harvest time and I help Tonya pick the remaining marble-size tomatoes, the last of the season, and a prized item. She asks the frequent question, "Do tomatoes grow year 'round in your country?" Her garden also produces potatoes, cucumbers and cabbages and has beds of strawberries and raspberries; a blueberry bush is there, but neither a pear nor apple tree like some dachas. All of this food is eventually toted to her apartment and cooked for immediate use or preserved.

Pointing to the corrugated tin roof of the dacha, I say, "It looks good." Responds Tonya, "It leaks."

Inside the dacha are garden tools, two dilapidated couches, gardening clothes, tin cans and galvanized buckets for transport, and the wooden table built by my father around which I sat with him, my mother, four sisters and two brothers. I recognize two ancient windows with double panes from my old home that give this dacha plenty of light. If the tar paper and wood dacha were winterized, it would be illegal; one residence per citizen is the rule to avoid any similarity to the capitalist system.

I tote a basket of the tomatoes on my head to the railroad stop. At the sound of a train whistle, a swarm of people hurry toward the station. The engineer waits patiently until the last person reaches the platform, a mob pulling, hauling and helping. Judging by the number of baskets and bags piling off the train in the city, I figure the 1976 growing season has been satisfactory.

On arrival at her apartment, Tonya does not use her unfamiliar refrigerator yet to advantage; canned goods inside it, and unwrapped fish-heads in the freezer. The old habit of using the balcony as an outdoor pantry, even in summer, persists.

And one morning, it is time to preserve some perishable berries. A frantic glass-jar pursuit – borrowing, counting, washing and dropping them. Food is scarce and expensive. War and starvation have left their mark.

My second visit to the dacha is on a Sunday; Marik driving Sasha, Tonya, Sondra, and me in his small car. A beautiful September day, crisp and cool, with leaves falling. We eat our picnic lunch of bread, cheese, tomatoes and chocolate in the dacha. Marik suggests a walk in the woods nearby to find mushrooms. Sondra and Sasha join him. After their return, Sondra tells the story of their safari:

It has been very dry. We walk and walk; tall trees and the sound of trains now and then. It's hard to believe this is Russia and the border with China a stone's throw away. Brambles catch on socks, sweaters, and jackets. Which way is the railroad? 'Papa, carry me,' pleads Sasha. Papa agrees. Are we north or south of where we started? Which way is the railroad? Lost! 'Wait here,' says Marik. He returns in fifteen minutes.

'I walked to the station Khekhiteir. We have to walk in the opposite direction.' Walk and walk along the embankment, then between the rails.

'Don't worry. No danger. You can hear a train far away.' More walking. No trains. No mushrooms. At last, there is the dirt road and Tonya's dacha.

'Thank goodness, you have all returned.' Warm greetings from Tonya and me.

The next day, Sondra must register at the passport office. Therefore, Tonya and I are soon seated with her in the waiting area on the third floor of an old building. Tonya, with asthma, has to catch her breath after climbing the steep stairs.

Because she had previously worked for the Voice of American in Washington, and speaks Russian, Sondra is aware of the long arm of the Soviet system and that foreigners, always under suspicion, are watched in public.

I am roaming around as usual while Sondra is looking out the window. I hear a male voice in accented English from the hall, "Does anyone here speak French?" The voice, now accompanied by a silent partner, reaches the waiting room.

The speaker, a rotund body with a balding head over a cherubic face, seats himself with a wheeze and a grunt, and addresses me in English. "I am looking for someone who speaks French." I cast a glance at my fluent French-speaking daughter. A scowl and a shake of her head.

"Er, French. That's a nice language. Do you speak French?" I ask. "Yes, I speak French," is the answer in Russian-accented English. I am here on business from Switzerland. My name is Ravelle, R-a-v-e-l-l-e. I am visiting my cousin here." He points to his companion. "I was born here but went to Switzerland long ago and have forgotten Russian."

"How do you talk with your cousin?"

"I don't but we understand each other." Then he proceeds to compare his situation to mine, and says that I am visiting my sister near the railroad station "with your daughter here. . . .

"You know a lot about me," I say.

After, "Yes, no. Not much," he reveals that he has followed me every place that morning.

"But I need someone to interpret here. I don't speak Russian. I want to go to Komsomolek-on-Amur and I want someone to ask the official here whether I can have permission to go there."

Turning to Sondra, "Can you ask whether I can go there?" In Russian, (later tranlated for me), she answers, "Mind your business." He seems taken back for someone who does not know Russian. Just by a tiny shift of pronoun in Russian, she knew that she could be incriminated.

She keeps filling out the necessary forms as he asks. "Where did you learn Russian?" I answer for her, "School, school. And you speak English very well." I may as well be diplomatic. After I make a few more positive statements, there are smiles.

Now the completed forms are handed to the official who mentions to Tonya the travel restrictions for foreigners. After wishing us a pleasant stay, he tells the "Swiss" visitor that the same restrictions apply to him. "But he doesn't speak Russian," says Sondra, as we leave. The official laughs and shows us out of his office. In front of the passport registration building, we exchange wishes for a happy stay.

CHAPTER 12

From Tonya's apartment, it is a short walk to that of my oldest sister, Motya. She is not as outgoing as Tonya and, I think, regards me as the foolish baby-brother who ran away to the enemy camp. Of course, all my remarks have to be translated for her and vice versa.

I refer to my memorable visit as a child to her home in the forest and the meal of bear meat. She shakes her head, saying, "I don't like to remember those times. They were very difficult. But now I have everything I need. It's good you left. You were little and skinny. You never would have survived." Her husband and two sons were killed during World War II; three sons and a daughter survive.

Tonya speaks of her sister's generosity regarding her living space and her money. Two teenage granddaughters share her one-room apartment, attending schools in Khabarovsk because their parents live out of the city. According to Tonya, "If another granddaughter needs to stay, she moves over and lets her stay. If someone needs money, she gives it to them. It means nothing to her."

The large TV in a corner has the programs Motya enjoys: old films, ballets, sports, especially soccer matches, Loto, and the news. The latest newspapers are stacked on a bureau near her door. Books arre stuffed in bookcases. Her sister says, "She reads everything, everything."

Tonya then tells her experience during the siege of Leningrad, the only relative who lived *The Nine Hundred Days* made famous by Harrison Salisbury. "How did we survive the Leningrad blockade? I have seen 200 grams of daily bread for two of us during the siege; only 10 percent of it flour. God forbid that it should happen to others as it happened to us. Quick death is nothing. Starvation is the worst thing in the world. My husband, to the end, never complained, even when he was lying in the hospital. He was only concerned with us. {Tonya and her son.}

"I remember now how the man in charge of our section of ration cards came to me and pleaded on his knees for me to give him the card of my deceased husband. He cried. He said now they would take his (my husband's card) away. But I didn't give it back to him. Now I remember it with shame. At one time, we had eight corpses nearby." She shakes her head. "How did we survive?" she repeats.

As the afternoon draws to a close, tea is poured from a silver-plated samovar on the kitchen table. Motya, missing her front teeth, sweetens her tea by cutting a hard candy in half - the paper wrapper still on it - with a knife the size of a machete. After she pops it in her mouth, she sips the sweetened tea.

Then I recalled the unusual coincidence that Tonya and I shared marine training: she as a graduate of the Leningrad Maritime Academy in 1934 and I as a graduate of a U.S. maritime training school in 1942,

Furthermore, she had worked ten years for the Red Cross that had eventually brought us together, working internationally. Tonya had been the superintendent of the Khabarovsk district, no doubt the source of some valuable connections!

Referring to Ivan and Mikhail, Tonya exclaims, "How they believed in the party. And what happened to them? Ivan got kicked out of the party when he was in his fifties . . with children and a wife. We had to send him money in Moscow." Ivan was accused by a worker of having been in the White Guard. To refute this charge, my mother wrote an appeal to the head of the General Party Committee, during Beria's time. "Ivan was rehabilitated in the late 1950s. A former

Bolshevik given that treatment! Who will stand for that?" concludes the embittered Tonya.

In 1929, when he was thirty and I, twenty, he answers one of my rare letters in which I had naively expressed my intention of going to the Soviet Union. Only tourists, newspaper reporters, scientists and a few politicians have a chance to receive permission, he wrote. The Iron Curtain was already in place over twenty years before Prime Minister Winston Churchill's metaphor.

Ivan's life was one of unbelievable intrigue and turmoil. At the beginning, he is sent to Latvia with the underground to recruit future members for the Communist Party; one of the group is a traitor. Ivan is sent to prison under the name of Rudolf Krassell with another man. He escapes and hides in Vladivostok under the protection of another Bolshevik. After obtaining a passport under another assumed name, he leaves for Khabarovsk. En route, his group is turned back because Khabarovsk is occuped by a White Russian army. Finally, after a month in a hospital with typhoid fever, he returns to Khabarovsk.

Now he is hiding either from the Japanese – their revolt began on April 5, 1920 – or from the anti-Communists. Again with a false passport, he works for two years as head of a state political agency in a city near the Chinese border,

Blagoveshchensk. Although he had graduated from the Khabarovsk Railroad Institute, he now enrolls at the Moscow Institute of Transport Engineers, leading to his employ as a civil engineer in railroad construction.

As for Mikhail, his life was the most tragic. At age 24, he graduates from the Leningrad Mining Institute, works for nine years as the assistant director and main engineer of a gold-mining operation in Kazakstan. During the Stalin era, he is pressured to fabricate evidence against a superior; he refuses to submit false evidence. Eight years in prison, plus five years without rights. He attempts to appeal in Moscow.

Tonya describes graphically our mother's last sight of him on the way to Magadan and the concentration camp – the Gulag: She saw him from the window of our house along the railroad tracks right here. Among all the prisoners with their heads shaved, she recognized him. 'Oh, Misha!' She was standing on a chair at the window and fell off when she saw him.

Misha died of malnutrition doing forced labor on the Kolymz Peninsula. He was buried far north of Magadan, and finally rehabilitated posthumously between 1949 and 1953.

A last photograph, given to me by Tonya, shows him, a hearty, well-built, curly-headed man in his early thirties, with Ivan and my mother.

My brothers paid dearly for their intense belief that the communist system was the answer to a better life for all.

"How they believed in the Party," exclaims Tonya. "Solizhenitsyn wrote the truth,".she continues. "Just like where Misha was. I would like to read *Gulag Archipelago;* someone here has a copy of it here, but they are sitting on it. I let people read my *Ivan Denisovich,"* (Tonya actually kept it in a locked suitcase with keepsakes and important documents.)

"Did you ever join the Communist Party," I ask Tonya.

"Thank heaven, I never did. What advantages does party membership give? No one believes in it now. {1976} People join the party for their self-interest. In 1954, I was asked to join the second time; Mother was at home, praying I wouldn't. I stood before the troika (a three-man tribunal). 'I don't feel I'm ready. Please give me a postponement.' Of course, Mother was happy when I told her.

"People see the injustice all around. . . . The future is uncertain. A lot of people are afraid of a repetition of what happened in the thirties. Good and loyal party members disappeared. It seems safer for many not to join the party. Lenin was good; Stalin was bad."

A quiet afternoon for the story of my parents' early life.

My father, Andrei Filoppovich Struchkov was born in the village of Nosini, southeast of Moscow. My mother, Pelageya, was a neighbor. As childen, Andrei at age eight, and Pelgeya at age ten, had their marriage arranged by their parents according to custom. Meanwhile, he worked as a shepherd and she in the fields tying wheat sheaves from 4:00 am to 10:00 pm for 10 kopeks a day. As teenagers, they marry in the town of their birth. In the next five years, Ivan, Motya and Mikhail are born.

About 1904 or 1905, my father leaves for Harbin, China, with a group of men, building houses with windows, a new feature. It was a long trip but many young people were seeking their fortunes in the Far East – like the Americans in the Far West. Shortly my mother joins him there with the three children. In Harbin, she takes in washing for a ruble a day.

Their next move is to a Russian town on the Chinese border by the Ussuri River where my father helps to build a church. The final move is to Khabarovsk where Tonya and I are born, in addition to Valya, the one with whom I had shared the sheepskin rug on the floor, (a victim of diphtheria at age 18) and Asya, whom I would eventually visit in Kiev. A family of seven children in a little four-room house that the czarist regime had given my father permission to build.

"You look like your father," says Tonya. If so, he was a muscular, stocky man with curly brown hair, brown eyes and a mustache.

Then Tonya brings my mother to life, quoting one of her sayings: 'Another man's brain is not one's own. Find one's own and go with it where you wish. '

My mother had little education; at her request, her father consented to provide two years of school. (My father had three.) With resilience and resourcefulness, she had survived economic hardship, and many personal tragedies, including my departure with no goodbyes. Moreover, she often had fear of losing her life at the hands of the Japanese or her own countrymen. A strong character and an inspiration to those who knew her. I, too, wish I had known her as an individual rather than a parent.

My time in Khabarovsk is short. But before I leave, Tonya puts a new light on a reason for my departure. She tells it as part of her life: In the late thirties, I was employed at a lamp-manufacturer's plant in Leningrad. I was told, 'You can no longer work here. You have a brother living abroad who fought on the side of the Whites during the civil war in Russia. We think you are dangerous.'

'How could a boy of ten have been fighting on any side? I pleaded in a letter to Stalin. 'This is simply not true, Comrade Stalin. He left with the American troops because he had been thrown out of the gimnasiya. Why had he been thrown out of the gimnasiya? Because his two older brothers were partisans, not Whites, and in 1920 in Khabarovsk, it was a crime to be a partisan, as you well know. My little brother was afraid to go home and face his family after he had been thrown out of school. No one told him that he was thrown out of school because of his brothers. So for three months, he didn't go home. He was ashamed. He spent most of his time watching the American soldiers who were encamped along the railroad. They fed him. They gave him a little uniform. Certainly, Comrade Stalin, our family has suffered because of our loyalty rather than our disloyalty. I request that I be reinstated in my job; I hope that you can help this misunderstanding.'

A few weeks later, Tonya is reinstated at the lamp factory with back pay.

A grand finale to the visit – pancakes eaten with salmon roe, strawberry jam to sweeten the tea, ravioli tidbits eaten in one bite and a paper-thin seven-layer cake baked in the electric oven that always rests on a kitchen chair.

I had occasionally bought a can of salmon roe or red caviar in New York City but now I learned that the salmon from which it comes is about a foot long. In Khabarovsk, during the fall salmon run, large quantities of the red caviar are available "with connections." Police road-blocks are set up, according to some reports, to check that people are not catching salmon illegally upstream for their personal consumption. It comes in the largest glass jars I have ever seen. Black caviar from sturgeon is for export.

It has taken a lifetime to mend and cross an international bridge of broken family ties. Determination and perseverance at one end and kindness and understanding at the other have succeeded in spite of circumstances initiated by me and, perhaps, by others.

Two eloquent lines of Robert Frost's poem, *The Road Not Taken,* come to mind:

I took the road less traveled by
And that has made all the difference.

THE END

About The Author

Constance W. Langtry graduated from Connecticut College, New London, CT, with a B.A. in English. Thirty-seven years later, she took graduate courses at the State University of New York at Oswego. For many years, she worked in New York City for various companies and New York University as an administrative assistant.

In 1957, she joined her husband, a Suez Canal pilot, in Port Said, Egypt, where she lived for five years. She has traveled extensively in Europe, Africa, the Middle East and the western part of Russia, in addition to Mexico and Canada.

Her home is in Wilmington, North Carolina.

www.ingramcontent.com/pod-product-compliance
Ingram Content Group UK Ltd.
Pitfield, Milton Keynes, MK11 3LW, UK
UKHW040017200726
13854UKWH00001B/241

9 780759 600713